ere is a little "Jethro" in all of us called *discontentment*. Linda so honestly
rtrays this truth and how we need to learn to like ourselves, "just how God
de us—lumps and all!" Every parent or grandparent needs to read this book
d THEN share it with their children!

Sue Hayes Fallin,
Author of **Gathering Manna**: *Finding God's Grace in Life's Wildreness*

nda has written a delightful story that teaches a valuable lesson not only to
ildren, but also adults. Relax and take a journey into this wonderfully written,
imsical story about Jethro, the frog.

Kathleen Sherwood,
Author of "McKenna" and "All My Tomorrows."

TATE PUBLISHING
& Enterprises

Tate Publishing is committed to excellence in the publishing industry. Our staff of highly trained professionals, including editors, graphic designers, and marketing personnel, work together to produce the very finest books available. The company reflects the philosophy established by the founders, based on Psalms 68:11,

"THE LORD GAVE THE WORD AND GREAT WAS THE COMPANY OF THOSE WHO PUBLISHED IT."

If you would like further information, please contact us:

1.888.361.9473 | www.tatepublishing.com

TATE PUBLISHING *& Enterprises*, LLC | 127 E. Trade Center Terrace

Mustang, Oklahoma 73064 USA

Jethro

Published in the United States of America

ISBN: 1-5988691-9-1

07.02.12

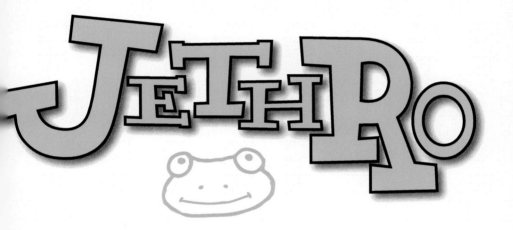

LINDA COURNOYER

TATE PUBLISHING & *Enterprises*

DEDICATED TO:

Daton, David & Elaina Marie

And for the glory of my precious Lord and Savior, Jesus Christ

Once upon a time, there was a very handsome frog named Jethro. He had beautiful green, bumpy skin that let the water run right off and kept him dry; big, strong hind legs that helped him to jump from lily pad to lily pad without falling into the water; eyes set just where a frog's eyes should be; ears just the right size for him; and a beautiful, deep voice that sang a song that sounded like this—"Ribbet, ribbet!" Then, there was his tongue. Oh, what a wonderful tongue he had! It was long and would jump out just when you least expected it, snatch a bug right out of the air, and stuff it in his mouth. Yes, indeed! Jethro was a very handsome frog—just as God had made him to be. But…Jethro was a most dissatisfied frog. He hated his beautiful bumpy green skin. He hated his eyes and ears. He hated his big, strong hind legs. He hated his voice that sang "ribbet, ribbet". But most of all, he hated that tongue that jumped out when he least expected it, stuffed a bug in his mouth, and just about scared the life out of him.

One day in the forest, he saw a deer jump over a tree that had fallen. What long, slender, beautiful legs that deer had. How graceful he was when he jumped. He seemed to just soar over the tree with those powerful legs. How Jethro would love to have legs like that instead of his big, fat legs!

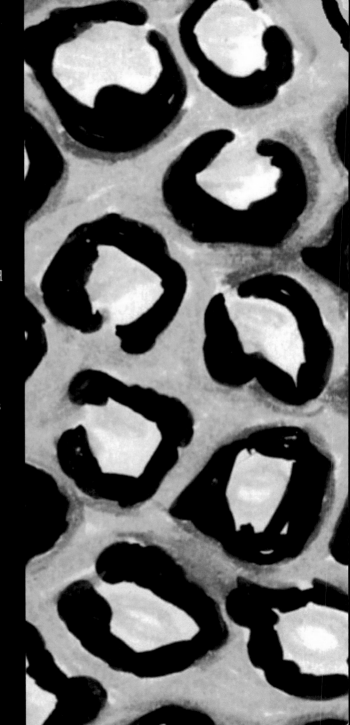

H e saw a leopard
with her
beautiful spotted
r. It looked so nice and
lt so soft. He thought,
My, wouldn't it be nice to
ve a gorgeous fur coat
ith all of those lovely spots
stead of my ugly, lumpy,
umpy, green skin. Why
wouldn't even feel the
rongest wind blowing
I was wrapped in such a
arm coat."

He dove to the bottom of the river and saw a crab scurrying around under the water. What fantastic eyes that crab had. They were on stalks! He was amazed as he watched one eye turn this way and the other eye that way. Why, if Jethro had those eyes, he could look in all directions at once.

He heard the birds singing beautiful melodies in the trees along the river bank and longed to be able to sing a song like their song. He was getting bored with singing just "Ribbet, ribbet". He wanted to add a few more notes and a few more words to his song.

He watched the chickens pecking their dinner from the ground and thought about how nice it would be to have a beak. Why, he could choose which bugs he wanted to eat. He could choose when he wanted to eat them instead of having that awful tongue that jumped out all the time—scaring him half to death and stuffing bugs in his mouth when he wasn't even hungry.

So, Jethro began to pray. He begged God to give him all the wonderful things he saw that the other creatures had. Day after day, hour after hour, he prayed and he prayed. Week after week without letup, he whined and he begged. One day, God had finally had enough. He decided to put a stop to this. He would answer Jethro's requests. He would give Jethro ALL that he had prayed and begged and nagged about—all at one time! And so, He did!

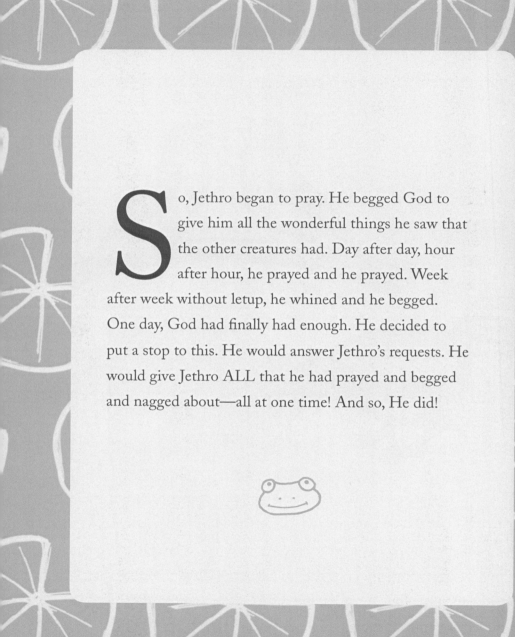

Oh, happy day! Jethro was beside himself! How special he must be! God had listened to him. God had heard and answered ALL of his prayers. What joy—what bliss Jethro's life would be. He now had a beautiful fur coat with spots like a leopard (no more ugly green bumps!), long slender legs like a deer (no fat legs for him!), eyes on stalks like a crab (nothing could sneak up on him now!), a bird's song (more notes—more words!), a chicken's beak (hallelujah—the tongue was gone!), and for good measure, God threw in a set of rabbit ears. Jethro was very, VERY happy! But…pretty soon, he found out that all the things he had prayed and begged and nagged for weren't as great as he had thought they would be.

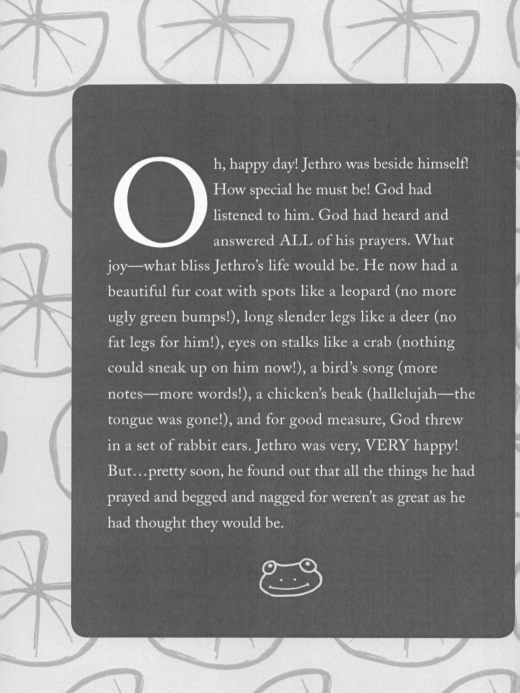

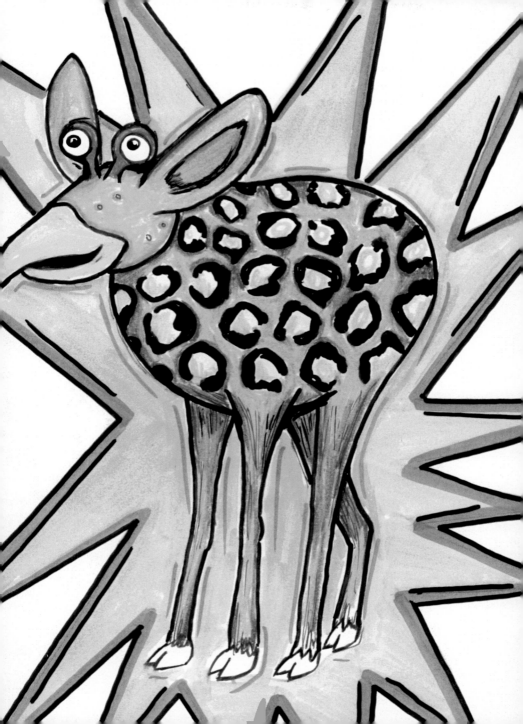

Oh, his long deer legs did help him to jump gracefully and with no effort, but he had been too busy praying and begging and nagging to look closely at the deer's legs. They had sharp pointed hooves at the end of them! So…every time he jumped from lily pad to lily pad, the hooves punched holes in them, and he wound up in the water.

His wonderful leopard's fur with the beautiful spots did keep out the cold wind; it did feel ever so soft; it did look really good on him; but it didn't shed the water like his old lumpy, bumpy, green skin—instead, it soaked up the water and held it next to his skin where it felt like ice. So ....this is how it went. He would leap to a lily pad, punch a hole in it, and wind up in the water—leap to the next lily pad, punch a hole in it, and wind up in the water—leap to the next lily pad, punch a hole in it, and wind up in the water. After a few times of leaping, punching and winding up in the water, Jethro was very, very wet and very, very cold.

It was true! He could hear ever so much better with his rabbit ears. He could tell if there were ten crickets or just two crickets chirping in the bushes. He could hear a snake slithering through the grass half a mile away. He could hear an eagle soaring in the air above the top of the highest mountain. He could hear….. he could hear……he could hear EVERYTHING! FOR MILES! ALL OF IT! and it was **LOUD!** What noise! What a racket! What a headache it gave him!

His eyes did twist this way and that way on stalks just like the eyes on the crab in the river, but he couldn't make them do what he wanted them to do. They just did what they felt like doing, and he had no control. All the twisting and turning, looking backwards and forwards at the same time, looking up while he was looking down, made him so dizzy that he got sick to his stomach.

His chicken's beak was great. It did let him choose which bugs he wanted, and it did let him choose when he wanted to eat. But his deer legs were so long that he couldn't reach the ground. What good did it do him to be able to choose which bugs he wanted and when he wanted to eat them? He couldn't reach the ground, so he couldn't get to the bugs.

His new song wasn't very good either. Oh, it did have more notes and more words—well, one more note and one more word. It sounded like this—"Chirp-ribbet. Chirp-ribbet."

You have never seen a sillier, sorrier, hungrier critter than Jethro was. You see, God made Jethro to be a very, very good frog—not a leopard, not a deer, not a crab, not a rabbit, not a bird or a chicken—just a very, very good FROG. Like Jethro, God has made each one of us to be the very best us we can be. Some of us can sing like a bird. Some of us can dance as gracefully as a deer jumps over a tree in the forest. Some of us are very beautiful like the leopard with her wonderfully spotted coat of soft fur. But, each of us is very special to God because He created us. He loves us just as we are—with the gifts that he chose especially for us. So, let's thank Him and be grateful every day for being just like we are instead of wishing we were like someone else.

listen|imagine|view|experience

AUDIO BOOK DOWNLOAD INCLUDED WITH THIS BOOK!

In your hands you hold a complete digital entertainment package. Besides purchasing the paper version of this book, this book includes a free download of the audio version of this book. Simply use the code listed below when visiting our website. Once downloaded to your computer, you can listen to the book through your computer's speakers, burn it to an audio CD or save the file to your portable music device (such as Apple's popular iPod) and listen on the go!

How to get your free audio book digital download:

1. Visit www.tatepublishing.com and click on the e|LIVE logo on the home page.
2. Enter the following coupon code:
   d52a-223e-7adc-034c-2aa5-bd6d-0a61-8ae5
3. Download the audio book from your e|LIVE digital locker and begin enjoying your new digital entertainment package today!